Kitty's Magic

Sooty the Birthday Cat

Kitty's magic

Sooty the Birthday Cat

Ella Moonheart

illustrated by Dave Williams

BLOOMSBURY
CHILDREN'S BOOKS
NEW YORK LONDON OXFORD NEW DELHI SYDNEY

BLOOMSBURY CHILDREN'S BOOKS
Bloomsbury Publishing Inc., part of Bloomsbury Publishing Plc
1385 Broadway, New York, NY 10018

BLOOMSBURY, BLOOMSBURY CHILDREN'S BOOKS, and the Diana logo
are trademarks of Bloomsbury Publishing Plc

First published in Great Britain in July 2018 by Bloomsbury Publishing Plc
Published in the United States of America in October 2018 by Bloomsbury Children's Books
www.bloomsbury.com

Text copyright © 2018 by Working Partners Ltd
Illustrations copyright © 2018 by Dave Williams

Bloomsbury books may be purchased for business or promotional use. For information on bulk
purchases please contact Macmillan Corporate and Premium Sales Department at
specialmarkets@macmillan.com

Library of Congress Cataloging-in-Publication Data
Names: Moonheart, Ella, author.
Title: Sooty the birthday cat / by Ella Moonheart.
Description: New York : Bloomsbury, 2018. | Series: Kitty's magic ; 6
Summary: After learning that Sooty, a local cat, does not know what
a birthday party is, Kitty decides to throw one for her, although Kitty's
visiting cousin Max is already keeping her very busy.
Identifiers: LCCN 2018024229 (print) | LCCN 2018030037 (e-book)
ISBN 978-1-68119-910-8 (paperback) • ISBN 978-1-68119-911-5 (hardcover)
ISBN 978-1-68119-912-2 (e-book)
Subjects: | CYAC: Cats—Fiction. | Shapeshifting—Fiction. | Magic—Fiction.
| Cousins—Fiction. | Parties—Fiction. | Grandmothers—Fiction. |
Japanese—England—Fiction. | England—Fiction.
Classification: LCC PZ7.1.M653 Soo 2018 (print) | LCC PZ7.1.M653 (e-book) |
DDC [Fic]—dc23
LC record available at https://lccn.loc.gov/2018024229

Typeset by RefineCatch Limited, Bungay, Suffolk
Printed and bound in the U.S.A. by Berryville Graphics Inc., Berryville, Virginia
2 4 6 8 10 9 7 5 3 1 (paperback)
2 4 6 8 10 9 7 5 3 1 (hardcover)

To find out more about our authors and books visit www.bloomsbury.com
and sign up for our newsletters.

Chapter 1

Kitty Kimura grinned as a car horn beeped outside her bedroom window. "He's here!" she cried, running downstairs and to the front door.

Kitty had been waiting all day for a very special visitor to arrive—her cousin Max. As Kitty flung the door open, she saw Max getting out of her mom and dad's car. Mr. and Mrs. Kimura had gone to pick Max up that afternoon. He lived on a farm in the countryside with Kitty's aunt and uncle, and this was his first visit to Kitty's home.

"Hi, Max!" Kitty waved excitedly.

"Hi, Kitty!" Max replied with a grin. "I can't believe I'm here!"

"And you're staying for the whole weekend," Kitty said. "Quick, come inside and see our house."

Kitty's mom laughed as she lifted Max's suitcase out of the trunk of the car. "Kitty, Max has had a long journey. Why don't we all have a drink and a snack before you start giving him the grand tour?"

"Don't worry! Grandma and I have got some snacks ready in the kitchen,"

Kitty said, leading Max into the front yard. "We've baked some strawberry tarts to help you feel more at home."

"Because I live at Strawberry Lane Farm," said Max. "Thanks, Kitty. Wow, your yard's so neat and tidy." He looked at the row of flowerpots lining the wall by the front door. "It's not a bit like our crazy farmyard, with all the muddy puddles and chickens everywhere!"

Kitty grinned as she remembered her visit to Strawberry Lane Farm three months ago. It was so funny to think that, at first, she and Max hadn't gotten along at all. But they soon found out they had lots in common—especially when it came to animals.

"How are Daisy and Star?" asked Kitty, thinking of Max's boisterous puppy and wise old farm cat. *They* hadn't gotten along very well with each other either, until Kitty had stepped in to help!

"They're best friends," said Max, grinning. "They spend every day together, chasing mice out of the barn. Mom and Dad say they've never seen a cat and dog be so friendly."

"You're so lucky, having a dog and a cat," Kitty said wistfully. "As well as all the chickens, ducks, pigs, cows, *and* horses!"

Kitty led Max inside and they sat down at the kitchen table with Mr. and Mrs. Kimura and Kitty's grandma, who also lived with them. As Grandma put warm strawberry tarts on everyone's plates, Max glanced around the kitchen.

"It feels strange being in a house with no animals at all," he said. "I'm so used to being surrounded by them on the farm. Why don't you have any pets, Kitty? I thought you might have a cat, seeing as they're your favorite."

"Kitty's allergic to cats," Kitty's mom explained as she poured them each a glass of juice.

"Yes," Kitty said. "If I spend too much time around them they make me sneeze." She looked at Grandma and the two of them shared a secret smile. The truth was, Kitty wasn't really allergic to cats. In fact, there were

actually *two* cats living in Kitty's house.
Both Kitty and Grandma had a special
gift—they could turn into cats! Kitty
loved her amazing power, especially
when it meant she could explore the
town late at night with all her cat friends.
But she and Grandma had to make sure
that no one found out, not even Kitty's

mom and dad, or their amazing power would be lost forever.

Once they'd all finished their strawberry tarts and juice, Kitty showed Max her bedroom and the cozy cot and sleeping bag her dad had set up for him in the corner.

"Would you like to go to the park?" she asked, once Max had unpacked his things. "Some of my friends from school will be there, and my best friend, Jenny. She really wants to meet you."

"Yes, please!" Max replied.

Grandma agreed to walk Kitty and Max to the park, which was a few streets away. Kitty skipped along beside them. She was so excited that Max was there—and even more excited to introduce him to her friends. *I only wish he could meet my cat friends as well as my human friends*, she thought, smiling to herself.

As they turned the corner toward the park, Kitty glimpsed three small, neat scratches at the bottom of a tree trunk. *The Cat Council symbol!* She quickly looked at Grandma, who nodded. *One of the cats in town has called a meeting for tonight*, Kitty thought. *I wonder who?*

The Cat Council was a meeting of all the local cats. Any cat could call a meeting whenever they wanted to talk about a problem, share some important cat news, or ask a question. The meetings were always held at night, once all the humans in town were fast asleep. Kitty and Grandma would need to sneak out of their house really quietly, making sure not to wake up Mom and Dad—or Max!

"Kitty, I forgot to tell you!" said Max as they walked into the park. "Mom and Dad gave me some extra pocket money last week for helping out on the farm, so I went to the candy store and bought the biggest bag I could. I thought we could have a midnight feast tonight. What do you think?"

"Uh . . ." Kitty hesitated. Usually the thought of a midnight feast with Max would have been great, but she had to be at the Cat Council meeting

tonight. How on earth would she manage to get away without being spotted if Max was going to stay awake until midnight?

Chapter 2

All evening, Kitty worried about how she was going to sneak away for the Cat Council meeting. She'd hoped Max might forget about the midnight feast, but he just kept getting more and more excited. Even Kitty's mom and dad had joined in the fun, making Kitty and Max some special chocolate milkshakes to have as an extra midnight treat. Kitty didn't know how she was going to get out of it!

She hoped that Max might get sleepy once they'd changed into their pajamas, but as they got into bed, her cousin seemed more wide awake than ever.

"This is awesome! I've never stayed up till midnight before," said Max, wriggling inside his sleeping bag. "Hey, maybe we could tell each other scary stories to keep ourselves awake."

"Good idea!" said Kitty. *Maybe if I tell Max the most boring story I can think of, he might fall asleep!* she thought. "I'll go first. Once upon a time there was a really normal man, who lived in a really normal town and he was—er—a bus driver."

Max frowned. "This isn't very scary, Kitty. I know! What if he was a *ghost* bus driver? And all the passengers on his bus were ghosts too."

Before Kitty knew it, Max was turning her boring story into a far more exciting one, and he was more wide-awake than ever! When the story had finished, Max told a spooky tale of his own, about a haunted farm full of ghostly pigs and sheep. Then, just when Kitty was hoping he might lie down and fall asleep, he rummaged around in his suit-case and pulled out a board game.

"Let's play this," he said. "It's a game where you play a witch or magician, and you've got to collect all the ingredients to cast your spell. It's great!"

Kitty's heart sank. She knew Max would never fall asleep if they played an exciting game. Out of the corner of her eye, Kitty watched the hands of her clock ticking by. It was ten to midnight, almost time for the Cat Council meeting. She was never going to get there in time. But then there was a knock on the door and Grandma poked her head into the room.

"Time for you to get some sleep," she said, giving Kitty a secret wink.

Kitty gave a huge sigh of relief. She should have known that Grandma would come to the rescue.

"But we haven't had our midnight feast yet," Max moaned.

"You can eat your treats tomorrow," Grandma said. "We have a busy day planned. You need to get a good night's sleep so you'll enjoy it."

"Okay." Max sighed as he snuggled down into his camp bed.

Kitty gave Grandma a relieved smile.

"Goodnight," Grandma said, with another wink at Kitty.

"Goodnight," Max and Kitty replied.

Max gave a loud yawn and closed his eyes.

Kitty held her breath for a few moments, then tiptoed over to check that he was really asleep. *At last!* she thought. *Time to go to the meeting.*

Very quietly, she pushed open her bedroom door and crept downstairs. It was dark and quiet in the house, but the kitchen curtains hadn't been drawn, so the room was brightly lit by the full moon. One of the kitchen windows was open just a crack. Kitty knew that Grandma must have left it like that on purpose, so that Kitty could sneak out!

She closed her eyes, took a deep breath, and softly said the special words that would turn her into a cat.

"*Human hands to kitten paws,*
Human fingers, kitten claws."

As she whispered the last word, Kitty felt a fizzing, tingling sensation sweeping through her nose. It went down her body, into her arms and fingers, and then right down into her toes and feet. Kitty always thought it felt like she was full of the bubbliest lemonade! She waited for the feeling to fade away, and when she opened her eyes again, she saw two familiar small white paws just beneath her nose. Kitty was a cat!

With a flick of her tail, Kitty crouched low, then sprang up onto the kitchen table. From there, she could leap to the windowsill and slip outside through the open window. Once she was in the yard, her ears and nose twitched with all the sounds and smells that her amazing cat senses could pick up.

Kitty ran over to her playhouse and jumped onto the roof, then leaped onto the backyard fence. She used her tail to balance as she trotted along it, past all the other yards in her street. Finally she arrived at the clearing in the wood where the Cat Council was always held. As she ran through the trees, she could see the other cats sitting in a circle, waiting for her.

"Ah, good!" meowed a small black cat with a white patch on her head as Kitty joined the circle. "You managed to get away without Max noticing."

The rest of the cats in the circle knew this cat as Suki, one of the oldest and wisest cats on the Council. But Kitty knew her in her human form too. To her, Suki was Grandma!

"Yes," Kitty panted. "Thank you for helping me!" Then she turned to the others. "Sorry I'm late, everyone." She took her place between Suki and a large tabby tomcat named Tiger. "My human cousin is staying at our house at the moment, and he's sleeping in my bedroom. I couldn't sneak out until he was asleep, in case he noticed—but it took a lot longer than I expected!"

"Don't worry, Kitty!" meowed a small gray cat named Misty, who was Kitty's closest cat friend.

"Yes!" added a fluffy blue-gray cat with a sparkly collar, who was called

Coco. "We know you've got to keep your special gift a secret from your humans. It must be very tricky for you and Suki sometimes."

"Thank you, everyone," said Kitty, purring gratefully to her friends.

"Well, now that we're all here, let's

begin!" announced Tiger. He was the leader of the Cat Council meetings—a job that suited him perfectly because he was kind and fair. "We'll start by saying the Meow Vow together."

The Meow Vow was a special rhyme that they all chanted at the start of every

Cat Council meeting. It was a promise to help out any cat who came to the Council with a question or a problem. Kitty had practiced saying the words to herself again and again after her very first meeting, and now she knew them by heart.

A hushed silence fell over the circle of cats, and then, all together, they began to say the special words.

"*We promise now,*
This solemn vow,
To help somehow,
When you meow."

When the vow had finished, Tiger looked around the circle. "Now, which cat called this meeting? Please come forward and tell us how we can help."

A young cat with glossy white fur with black smudges stepped nervously into the middle of the circle. "I'm Sooty," she said, her voice trembling. "And I called the meeting because something really terrible happened at my house yesterday—and I'm really worried it might happen again!"

Chapter 3

A shocked murmur rippled around the circle. All the cats wanted to know about the terrible thing that Sooty had seen.

"Do you think you could tell us what happened, Sooty?" Kitty asked gently.

Sooty nodded and took a deep breath. "Well, first of all, my human,

Sophie, went out shopping for my favorite sardines."

"That doesn't sound terrible," purred Tiger. "That sounds delicious."

"It's what happened next that was terrible," Sooty meowed. "While Sophie was out of the house, lots of other humans arrived. They were all so noisy, laughing and chattering away. Then they pinned lots of big, colorful things to the ceiling, and they filled the whole kitchen with human food. Then the terrible thing happened."

A kitten named Ruby squeaked anxiously. "I don't know if I can listen. This sounds like it's going to be scary!"

"All the humans got into hiding places around my house," said Sooty. "Some of them hid behind the sofa, some hid behind the curtains, and some even crouched under the table. They stayed very still and very quiet—until Sophie came home. And then, when she walked through the door, they all leaped out and started shouting. I was so scared I nearly jumped out of my fur!"

Kitty thought she was beginning to understand what had happened at Sooty's house. "Can you remember what they were shouting, Sooty?" she asked.

"It was very strange!" meowed Sooty. "First of all, they yelled, 'SURPRISE!' And then they shouted, 'HAPPY BIRD-DAY!' over and over again. Some of them even started singing it too. But there weren't even

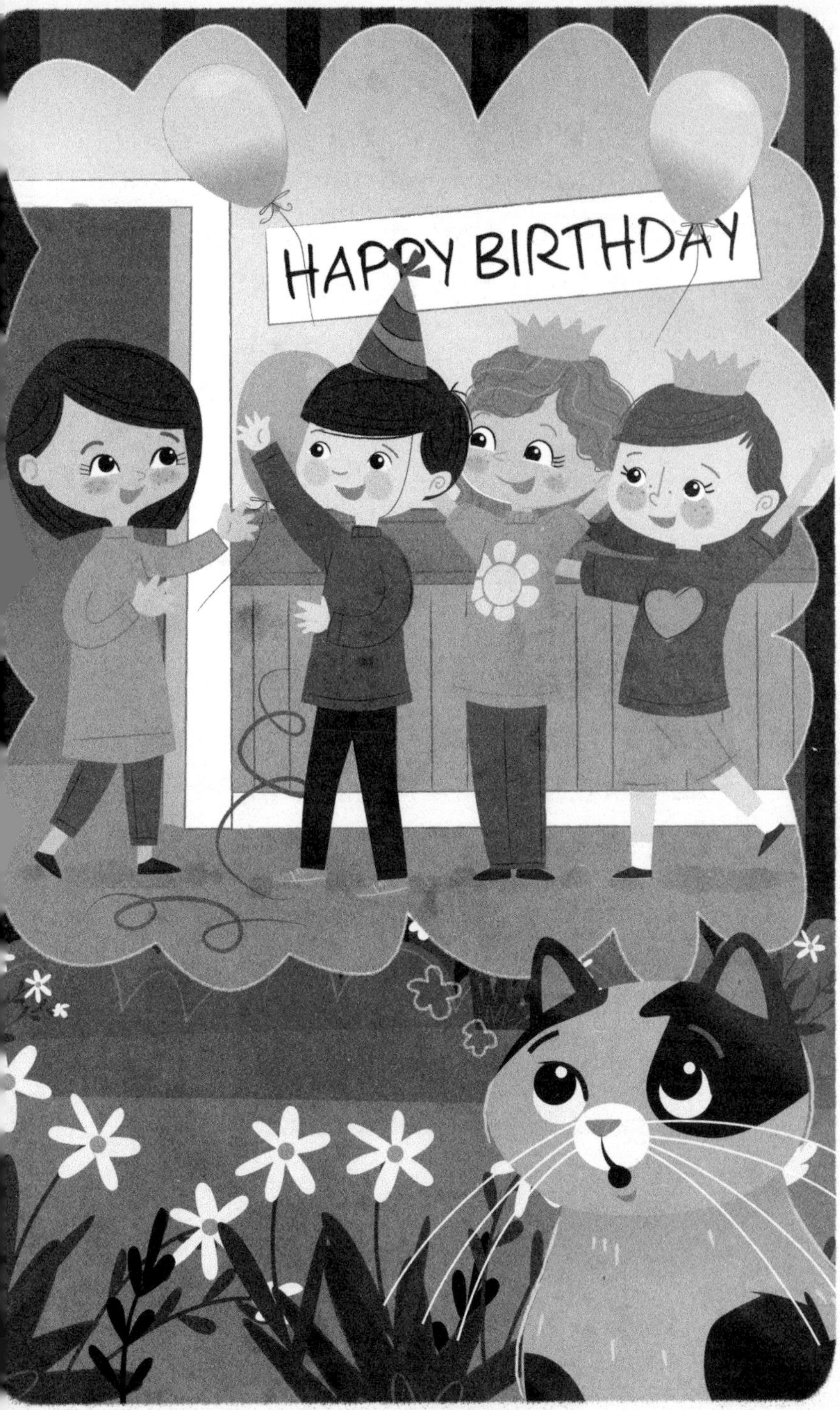
HAPPY BIRTHDAY

any birds there—and there were none in our yard either, because I'd chased them all away that morning."

Kitty began to laugh. Sooty and the other cats stared at her.

"What's so funny, Kitty?" asked Misty, looking puzzled.

"It's okay, Sooty," said Kitty. "The humans who came to your house when Sophie was out weren't doing anything scary or terrible. They were doing something nice. They were throwing Sophie a surprise birthday party!"

"What's a birthday party?" Sooty meowed.

"It's something humans do for their friends or families sometimes, to celebrate the day they were born,"

Kitty explained. "They usually have lots of nice food and drinks, and balloons and decorations. That must be what they were putting on the ceiling—balloons!"

"But why did they shout HAPPY BIRD-DAY?" asked Sooty.

"They were saying HAPPY BIRTH-DAY, not HAPPY BIRD-DAY!" explained Kitty, giggling. "And there's a special Happy Birthday song too— that must be what you heard them singing to Sophie."

Some of the cats round the circle began nodding their heads eagerly. "Now that I come to think of it, Kitty, my human had a birthday party once too!" meowed a slim, hairless cat called Pinky. "There were balloons up in our house—I didn't like them much, because I touched one with my claw by accident and it made a really loud bang. And there was lots of music and singing, and a great big cake!"

"Oh, birthday parties sound fun," meowed Ruby excitedly. "I hope my human has one soon!"

To Kitty's surprise, Sooty looked

angry. "Well, I don't think they're fun at all," she hissed. "They're noisy and busy and too hot. And I especially don't like surprises. I like everything to stay the same, all the time!"

Just then, an owl swooped over the circle and gave a loud hoot.

Sooty gasped, her black-and-white fur standing on end. "See!" she cried. "Surprises are scary! They make me jump."

"Sooty, that was just an owl," Tiger said kindly, but Sooty wouldn't listen.

"I'm going home to bed now," she announced, marching out of the circle. "I don't want any more nasty surprises!"

The other cats watched as Sooty ran out of the clearing. "Oh dear!" said Kitty anxiously. "That didn't go very well. I thought that if I explained about surprise birthday parties to Sooty, she'd realize there was nothing to feel scared about."

"Don't worry, Kitty. That's just how Sooty is—she's never liked surprises," said Misty.

Kitty noticed that Suki was sitting very quietly, looking thoughtful. "What is it, Grandma?" she asked.

"Oh, I was just thinking about Sooty's mom. We were good friends when we were a bit younger, you see. And I seem to remember it being around this time of year that Sooty was born." Suki nodded firmly. "Yes, I'm sure of it. In fact, I think it must be Sooty's birthday in a couple of days."

Kitty's eyes widened. "That's just given me a great idea," she said. "Why don't we throw Sooty a birthday party of her very own? If we make sure that it's tons of fun, we can show her that surprises can be a good thing after all."

"That's a wonderful idea!" meowed a fluffy gray cat named Smoky.

"Can we all help, Kitty? I've never thrown a party before!" said a cat called Emerald.

"Of course! In fact, I'll need everyone's help to keep it a secret from Sooty —and from my human family too," said Kitty. "My cousin Max is staying with me for a few more days, so I'll need to be extra careful that he doesn't see me changing between my cat and human forms. If he does, I'll lose my powers forever!"

"We'll do everything we can, Kitty," promised Misty. The rest of the circle meowed in agreement.

"Thanks, everyone," purred Kitty.

The cats said goodnight to one another and began to slip back home. Kitty, Suki, and Misty left together, trotting quickly through the clearing and heading for their street. But as they reached the edge of the woods, Kitty saw two dark shadows lurking beneath a tall tree.

"Wait a minute!" hissed Misty, spotting them too. "I think I know those cats . . ."

"It's Claws and Fang!" whispered Kitty. "Those Persian cats who tried to bully us. I haven't seen them around here since then—but it looks like they're back. I hope they didn't hear what we were talking about!"

"Let's not go near them," whispered Misty. "I don't want to get chased again."

But just as she spoke, the two fluffy white cats spotted them. For a moment, they froze—and then they ran off.

"That's weird," Misty whispered. "This time they were running away from us."

Kitty frowned. "I don't trust those cats," she meowed. "I just hope they're not up to something!"

Chapter 4

The next day, Kitty's mom took Kitty, Max, and Jenny into town.

"This probably seems really weird to you," said Max as they walked down the main street, "but I hardly ever go shopping when I'm at home. We don't live near a town, and Mom and Dad get most of our groceries from the farmers' market. This feels so big to me!"

Kitty and Jenny grinned. Their town was actually pretty small, with only a post office, a bookstore, a super-market, a café, and the tiny shop selling Japanese trinkets that was owned by Kitty's mom and dad. It was funny that Max thought it felt big!

"I need to go to the post office first," said Kitty's mom, waving a stack of letters.

As they all walked inside, Kitty spotted a display next to the birthday cards and stamps. It was a table piled high with different-colored balls of wool. There was a sign pinned up above it, saying "KNITTING WOOL— SPECIAL OFFER TODAY!"

That would make a perfect birthday

present for Sooty, Kitty thought. Every cat she knew loved playing with wool, tangling it around in their paws. She felt in her pocket for her purse and quickly checked to see how much pocket money she had inside. There was enough for a ball of wool! But how would she explain it to Jenny and Max?

"Oh, look," she said brightly. "Wool. Just what I needed. I—uh—I'm going to start knitting."

"Knitting?" Jenny said, staring at Kitty. "I didn't know you liked knitting, Kitty."

Kitty thought quickly. "Well—uh—my grandma loves knitting, so I thought it would be nice if we had the same hobby. She's going to teach me how to make a scarf for winter," she added.

"Oh! That sounds like fun," said Jenny. "Do you think she'd teach me how to make a scarf too?"

Oh no! thought Kitty. She was fairly sure Grandma had never knitted anything in her life. She'd just have to hope that Jenny would forget all about it—and wouldn't mention it to Grandma!

She quickly paid for a ball of pink wool and stuffed it into her coat pocket. Next, they headed to the supermarket.

"Why don't you all go and pick out a nice treat from the candy aisle?" Kitty's mom said.

Kitty, Jenny, and Max walked eagerly

through the supermarket toward the candy aisle, but on the way, Kitty caught sight of something in the canned food section: a stack of blue cans with bright red labels on them. *Sardines*. Kitty thought of what Sooty had said at the Cat Council meeting. Sardines were Sooty's favorite.

When she was in her human form, Kitty didn't like sardines very much at all. But when she was a cat, she thought they were delicious—just like every other cat she knew. Some cans of sardines would make the perfect food for Sooty's surprise party!

Without thinking, she reached out and grabbed three cans of sardines from the shelf. Max and Jenny stared at her.

"Kitty, what are you doing?" asked Jenny.

"Sardines—yuck!" said Max, making a face.

"I like them!" Kitty said quickly, feeling her cheeks flush pink.

"Well, if you want to buy those, Kitty, you'll have to do it with your candy money," said Mrs. Kimura. "They're quite expensive, you know. And I hope you're going to eat them. Your dad and I don't like sardines, and neither does your grandma."

Kitty thought of the delicious chocolate and caramel bar she'd been planning to buy, and her heart sank. She couldn't believe she was about to buy sardines instead of candy! But she

knew she needed special cat treats for the surprise party. "I'll eat them," she promised, putting the cans into her mom's shopping basket.

"You're crazy, Kitty!" laughed Max as they walked over to the register to pay.

"Are you feeling okay?" whispered Jenny.

Kitty smiled and nodded.

Once Mrs. Kimura had paid for their shopping, they headed outside. By the exit, one of the shop assistants was stacking up a pile of empty cardboard boxes.

Those would be perfect for the cats to play in at the party! thought Kitty. Cats loved hiding in cardboard boxes, batting them around with their paws, and using them to scratch their claws against. She knew Jenny and Max would think she was acting even crazier if she asked for some —but she had to make this party fun for Sooty.

"Excuse me," she said to the shop assistant, "do you think I could have some of those boxes?"

"Help yourself!" said the girl. "I'm just leaving them here for the recycling van to pick up. What do you need them for?"

"Yes, Kitty—what *do* you need them for?" asked Kitty's mom, frowning.

"I need them for—er—a doll's house," Kitty explained. "I want to build my own doll's house out of cardboard! I saw someone doing it on TV."

Jenny looked puzzled. "But you don't have any dolls," she said. "You've never really been into dolls, Kitty— you've always liked animals best."

Kitty really wished she'd thought of a better reason for taking the boxes. Jenny knew her too well! "It just seemed like a fun thing to do," she said, shrugging.

Luckily, her mom changed the subject. "Time to go home for some lunch," she said as Kitty picked up a couple of the cardboard boxes.

When they got back to Kitty's house, Jenny gasped. "Oh, look at those gorgeous cats!"

Kitty peered down the street and saw the white Persian cats, Claws and Fang, sitting outside her house, meowing noisily. Jenny rushed over and started stroking them, followed by Max.

"You're so fluffy and beautiful!" said Jenny, tickling Fang's chin. "I wonder where you live. Aren't they lovely, Kitty?"

Kitty hung back, not wanting to

stroke the cats. They'd been so mean to her and Misty—but there was no way she'd be able to explain that to Max or Jenny!

It's strange that I've seen them twice in two days, she thought to herself. *I wonder why they're here—and what they want...*

* * *

That night, Kitty lay awake until she was sure Max was fast asleep. Very quietly she climbed out of bed, tiptoed downstairs to the kitchen, and changed into her cat form. She was going to go and pay Misty and some of the other cats a nighttime visit and tell them what she'd managed to buy today for Sooty's party.

As the fizzing, bubbling feeling in her body faded, she jumped onto the kitchen table and over to the windowsill. But as she leaped outside and landed in the yard, her fur immediately began to prickle. Her cat senses were telling her that another cat was close by. Or *two* cats!

Waiting next to her playhouse, and looking right at her, were the two Persians, Claws and Fang.

Kitty gasped and took a hasty step back. *If I move really quickly, I might be able to jump back inside before they can get to me*, she thought. Kitty wasn't a scaredy-cat, but she knew that Claws and Fang didn't like her much.

But before she could make her escape, the Persians opened their mouths and began meowing, wailing and screeching as loudly as they could.

Kitty stared at them. "What are you doing?" she hissed. "Be quiet—you're going to wake up the whole street!"

She glanced at her house and to her horror, she saw the light in her bedroom flick on, and the window open. Max's face appeared, yawning.

"Kitty?" he called sleepily. "Where are you? What's that noise?"

"Now look what you've done!" Kitty hissed at the cats. Quickly she leaped back through the kitchen window. As soon as her paws touched the kitchen floor, she began to meow the words that would turn her back into a human.

"Kitten paws to human toes,

Kitten whiskers, human nose."

She closed her eyes as the magical fizzing feeling spread through her claws and the pads of her feet, through her tail, and into her ears and whiskers. Just as the feeling began to fade, she heard the thump of footsteps coming downstairs and the creak of the kitchen door opening.

Please, please, please let me have changed back in time! Kitty thought.

"Kitty! I wondered where you were," said Max, stepping into the kitchen and switching on the light. "Why are you down here by yourself in the middle of the night—and with the lights off?"

Kitty's heart thudded with relief. She was human again—just in time! If Max had caught the final seconds of her transformation from cat to human, she would have lost her magical gift forever.

"I heard those cats yowling," she explained, nodding her head toward the yard. "It's the fluffy white Persians we saw earlier. They woke me up, so

I came downstairs to—uh—to make sure they hadn't caught a mouse in our yard. But it's okay—I think they were just play-fighting."

Max nodded. "They woke me up too," he said. "Oh well—I suppose we should go back to bed before your mom and dad wake up."

"Good idea," agreed Kitty.

As she followed her cousin up the stairs, she shook her head with disbelief. She had never been so close to being caught before. *I can't let that happen ever again*, she told herself firmly. *I can't risk losing my gift, no matter what!*

Chapter 5

The next morning, Kitty slipped downstairs before Max was awake. She needed to speak to Grandma without him hearing.

"Good morning, Kitty," said Grandma as Kitty walked into the kitchen. She was making a cup of tea to drink with her breakfast. "Did you sleep well?"

"Not really, Grandma!" said Kitty. Quickly, she explained what had happened the night before.

"Goodness!" replied Grandma. "You did have a lucky escape."

"The worst thing was that I couldn't go out and meet Misty or any of the other cats," explained Kitty. "So I haven't been able to tell them the plan for Sooty's party this afternoon. I have to go out today and find them all—but I don't know how I'll manage to slip away without Max noticing."

Grandma took a sip of her tea and looked thoughtful. "I know!" she said. "I'll take Max to see your mom and dad's shop. He hasn't visited it yet. We'll tell him you're working on a school project so you need to stay at home. While we're out, you can turn into your cat form and sneak away."

"Good idea. Thanks, Grandma!" said Kitty, smiling.

After breakfast, Kitty went up to her bedroom and grabbed her schoolbag and pencil case. She plunked them down on the kitchen table and took out some books. "I'm afraid I've got some homework to do," she said to Max, pretending to look annoyed. "So I've got to stay home this morning. But don't worry, Grandma's going to take you to see my mom and dad's shop."

"Oh, okay!" said Max. "Maybe we'll see you later, though?"

"Definitely," said Kitty.

When Grandma and Max left, Kitty watched through the living-room window until they reached the end of the street. Then she closed her eyes and spoke the magic words.

"*Human hands to kitten paws,*
Human fingers, kitten claws."

The bubbling, tingling sensation fizzed through Kitty's body. As soon as it stopped she was a cat once more! She gave her tail a swish and her back paws a stretch, then she jumped through the kitchen window and ran toward the next street. Three of the cats from the Council lived there. They could help her spread the word about the party.

Kitty was in luck. As soon as she turned the corner onto Cherry Street, she spotted Coco, Boots, and Patch sitting in a pool of sunlight.

"Hi, Kitty!" purred Coco.

Kitty ran up to the three cats and gently bumped foreheads with them, which was a special cat way of saying hello.

"I'm so glad I've found you," she meowed. "Sooty's party is going to be this afternoon, at three o'clock. That's when the bell on the town-hall clock chimes three times," she added.

"I'm so excited about this party!" meowed Boots, a huge Maine Coon cat with big paws and long black fur. "Where's it going to be, Kitty?"

Kitty had thought very hard about
the best place to have a party. It needed
to be somewhere quiet, where humans
wouldn't go, with lots of space for the
cats to roll around and play. "The empty
patch of woodland at the back of the
park," she replied. "There are some big

rosebushes that we can all hide behind, and jump out to surprise Sooty."

"Can we help at all?" asked Patch hopefully. Patch was a small scruffy gray cat.

"Yes, please!" said Kitty. "I'm going to head this way to tell all the cats I can find." She waved a paw toward the end of the street. "Would you mind going around the other side of town, and telling the cats who live there?"

Patch nodded his head eagerly. "Of course."

"What about Sooty? How are we going to make sure she gets to the party without ruining the surprise?" asked Coco.

"Leave that to me," said Kitty.

Then she padded away from her friends, heading for the part of town where Sooty lived. On the way she passed several more cats, and every time, she stopped to tell them the plan. "Spread the word—but make sure you don't tell Sooty!" she meowed.

Kitty found Sooty playing with a ball near her house. "Hi, Sooty!" she called. "I've been looking everywhere for you."

"Why, what's happened?" asked Sooty.

"There's going to be an emergency meeting of the Cat Council at three o'clock today," Kitty explained. "And it's not in the usual place. It's going to be in the woodland behind the park instead. Just behind the rosebushes."

"I know where you mean," meowed Sooty. "I'll be there. I hope everything's okay, Kitty. I've never heard of a Cat Council meeting being called in the daytime before."

"Don't worry, it's nothing bad," Kitty said. "See you this afternoon." As she trotted away, she felt a tingle of

excitement in her tummy. Everything was going according to plan so far!

On her way back home, Kitty slipped over Jenny's fence and into Jenny's yard. There was one cat she hadn't told about the party plan yet—Misty! Her friend was lying on Jenny's trampoline, snoozing in the sunshine. Kitty gave a loud meow to wake her up.

"Kitty, you startled me!" giggled Misty, jumping down from the trampoline with a soft thud of her paws. "Do you want to play?"

"Yes, but first of all I've got to tell you about Sooty's party!" meowed Kitty. She started to explain the plan to Misty. But then the back door of Jenny's house opened, and two people stepped out into the garden.

Kitty stared in horror. The first person coming outside was Jenny—but the second, to her surprise, was Max!

"What's my cousin doing here?" she hissed to Misty. "He's supposed to be at my mom and dad's shop with my grandma."

"I want you to meet my cat, Misty," Jenny said to Max. "She's out here in the garden. She's so—oh, look, she's made a friend!"

Kitty felt all the fur on her body prickle. Max and Jenny were looking right at her! *It's okay*, she told herself. *They don't know it's you.*

"What a cute cat," Max said, walking

over to Kitty and crouching down. "That's weird. I feel like I've seen her somewhere before."

Kitty froze. If Max caught sight of the silver pendant hanging from her collar, he might realize that it matched the necklace Kitty wore when she was in her human form. And then he might realize that he'd seen her in her cat form before—when she was staying at his farm! She had to get away—and quickly! As Max reached out a hand to give her a stroke, she dashed away and onto the fence.

That was far too close—again, Kitty thought to herself as she jumped down on the other side.

Chapter 6

Kitty raced through her neighbors' yards and leaped over the fence into her own. Glancing around quickly to make sure no one could see, she whispered the magic words on her collar and transformed back into a girl. Then she opened the back door and stepped inside the house. "Grandma!" she called. "Grandma, are you here?"

"Kitty!" replied Grandma, bustling into the kitchen. "I've got some good news. Max isn't here. Jenny and her mom came into the shop while we were showing Max around, and they invited him to go and play out in Jenny's yard for a few hours. So that means he'll be kept busy while you're throwing the party for Sooty."

"I know Max is at Jenny's, Grandma. I was just there too!" said Kitty. She explained what had happened and how close Max had been to spotting her collar.

"Oh, no! I never thought that you'd be there too," said Grandma, shaking her head. "I'm sorry, Kitty. And I'm so glad you got away in time."

"It's okay, Grandma. It wasn't your fault," Kitty replied. "And you're right—at least we don't have to worry about Max now. We can concentrate on making Sooty's party perfect instead."

She checked the clock on the kitchen wall. "In fact, we'd better start taking all the party things to the park," she said. "It begins in an hour!"

Grandma and Kitty put the wool and sardines that Kitty had bought in a bag, along with some extra cans of tuna and a carton of fresh cream that Grandma had bought that morning. Then Kitty tucked the cardboard boxes under her arm while Grandma carefully pulled a large box out of the fridge.

"What's that?" Kitty asked.

"You'll see when we get there!" Grandma said, smiling.

When they got to the park the playground was really busy, and Kitty spotted some of her friends on the swings. Quickly she and Grandma ducked behind some trees and made their way to the empty patch of woodland at the far end of the park. It was hidden behind a row of thick rosebushes, which they carefully squeezed through.

"This is going to be perfect!" said Kitty, looking around.

She put the cardboard boxes on the grass so that the cats could jump in and out of them easily. Then Grandma opened the cans of tuna and sardines and scooped the fish into bowls, and

Kitty poured the cream into a big saucer.

"The cats are going to love this!" she said.

Kitty hadn't brought any balloons to the party, because she knew that if any of them popped, Sooty would hate the loud noise. But she had brought some party games. She'd wrapped a toy mouse inside lots of layers of newspaper, so that the cats could play pass the parcel.

"What a good idea, Kitty," Grandma said as Kitty put it on the grass, ready for the cats to play with when they arrived.

"Now will you tell me what's in the big box, Grandma?" asked Kitty.

Grandma chuckled and took the lid off the box. "It's a birthday cake," she said, showing Kitty.

"It doesn't look like any birthday cake I've ever seen before!" said Kitty, staring at it.

"I made it specially," Grandma explained. "It's made from cat treats."

Kitty giggled. Then she heard the town hall clock chiming. "It's quarter to three!" she exclaimed. "Everyone's going to be here soon—including Sooty! We'd better change, Grandma."

Grandma nodded and smiled. She whispered the secret words and turned into her cat form, and Kitty did the same.

And they were just in time! As

Kitty opened her eyes again, she saw the first cats begin to trot through the rosebushes.

"We're here for the party. We can't wait!" squeaked an excited ginger kitten.

"Thank you for coming!" meowed Kitty.

The cats purred happily as they saw the treats and games that Kitty and Grandma had prepared. One by one, more cats arrived.

Finally, Kitty heard the town hall clock chime three times. "That's it!" she whispered. "It's three o'clock! Everyone, get in your hiding places."

The cats all scampered off to hide in the bushes at the other side of the clearing.

Kitty felt nervous as she waited for Sooty to arrive. She really hoped she'd like her surprise. Kitty held her breath as a paw stepped through the rosebushes, and Sooty's face appeared. She looked at the party things and frowned in confusion.

"Hello?" she called. "Where's the Cat Council meeting?"

"Surprise!" meowed Kitty, jumping out from her hiding place. "Happy birthday, Sooty!"

Sooty gasped and her eyes widened as the other cats jumped out too, all meowing, "Happy birthday!"

"It's your birthday, Sooty!" explained Suki. "And Kitty thought it would be nice to throw you a party."

"I hope you like it," added Kitty. Her nerves grew. What if Sooty hated the party—just like she hated all surprises?

To her relief, Sooty gave a loud, happy purr. "I can't believe it!" she said. "Is all this for me?" She padded around the clearing looking at all the fun treats and food. "Oh wow, sardines. My favorite!"

The cats pounced on the fish and the cream, and then Grandma showed them the special birthday cake. Kitty taught the cats the words to "Happy Birthday" and they all meowed along. Then Kitty rolled the ball of pink wool to Sooty. "This is your birthday present!" she told her.

Sooty immediately began to tangle the wool with her claws. "I love it!" she purred. "Thank you, Kitty!"

Next it was time to start the party games. Kitty asked the cats to sit in a circle—just like they would at a Cat Council meeting. Then the cats began playing pass the parcel, using their noses and their paws to roll the parcel along the grass. Kitty meowed a tune, as they didn't have any music.

"Remember, when I stop the tune, whoever has the parcel takes a layer of paper off!" she told them.

But then suddenly all the cats' ears pricked up.

"Someone's coming!" hissed Misty. "I can hear cat paws, and . . ."

"Human feet!" added Suki.

Kitty looked at the party things scattered everywhere, and her heart sank. They would never tidy up in time. Whoever was coming was going to discover the party!

Misty's nose twitched. "Wait a minute. I know that smell," she

meowed. "Kitty, I think it's Claws and Fang!"

As she spoke, the two Persians burst through the rosebushes. The cats scattered out of their circle, hissing, as the Persians ran into the middle.

"We *knew* you were up to something," Fang hissed at Kitty.

"So we decided to spoil your fun," Claws said.

"We've led your cousin to the park," Fang said with a nasty grin on his face. "He's right behind us—and he's going to find out all about your cat party!"

"Yes, your secret's about to be found out," added Claws, "and you'll never be able to turn into a cat again!"

Chapter 7

Kitty's mind raced. She had to do something—and fast!

"Quick, Grandma. Behind those trees!" she meowed.

She and Grandma raced to hide behind some tall oak trees just as Max stepped through the bushes and into the clearing. "Wow!" Kitty heard him say. "What's going on?"

Kitty and Grandma whispered the words that would change them back into humans and waited as the bubbling, tickling feeling took over. As soon as they'd transformed back, they nodded at each other and stepped out from behind the trees.

"Kitty!" cried Max. "What are you doing here?"

"Surprise!" said Kitty, smiling. "Welcome to our cat party."

Out of the corner of her eye, Kitty saw Claws and Fang look at each other in shock. The Persians definitely hadn't been expecting that!

"Cat party?" repeated Max.

"We knew you were missing all the animals on your farm!" Grandma said, winking at Kitty. "So we decided to throw you a special party where you could meet all the cats in town. I see you've already met Claws and Fang," she added, pointing to the fluffy white Persians—who were now growling angrily.

"They were waiting outside the house again when I got back from Jenny's," explained Max. "They were meowing really loudly, and they started pulling at my trousers with their claws—it was as if they wanted to tell me something important! So I followed them to the park—but I was never expecting *this*." He stared around at the bowls of fish and cream, and grinned as he saw the ball of wool Kitty had bought

from the post office. "I recognize that!" he laughed. "Now I see what you were up to on our shopping trip, Kitty. The wool, the sardines, and the cardboard boxes—they were all for the cat party!"

"Right," laughed Kitty. *Thank goodness for that!* she thought to herself. *Now at least Max doesn't think I'm crazy!*

"Would you like to meet the cats?" she asked, sitting down on the grass.

"Yes, please!" Max replied eagerly. He sat down next to her and grinned as three cats trotted up to him and rubbed their furry heads against his knees.

"This is Sooty, Coco, and Boots," Kitty told him. "Then over here we've got Ruby, Tiger, and Shadow."

"I can't believe you've got so many

cat friends," Max said, stroking each cat as Kitty introduced them.

Suddenly, Kitty realized that she had to make sure Max didn't tell her mom and dad about this party.

"I keep it a secret," she explained, "because Mom and Dad worry about my allergies. I don't think they'd like me spending so much time with cats, so don't say anything, will you?"

"Of course not," said Max, picking up Sooty and giving her a hug. "Your secret's safe with me."

As Max and Grandma played with the cats, Kitty turned and saw Claws jumping in and out of one of the cardboard boxes, while Fang batted the toy mouse from the pass-the-parcel game around in his paws. They were both purring—and they seemed to be having fun! She walked over to them cautiously and knelt down beside them. To her surprise, Fang only hesitated for a moment—then came over and rubbed his face against her hand.

"Can we *please* be friends now?" she asked.

Claws purred in reply. Kitty couldn't tell what he was saying—but she was sure he was saying yes. It looked as if the Persians were having so much fun at the party, they'd decided to try being nice. "I'm so glad!" Kitty whispered, giving them both a stroke.

She felt another nudge at her elbow, and turned to see Sooty, who'd come over for a cuddle too. Sooty had crumbs of birthday cake stuck in her whiskers and a tangle of pink wool wrapped around her tail.

Sooty meowed and rubbed her head against Kitty's arm. Kitty knew she was saying "Thank you."

Kitty scooped Sooty up into her lap and stroked her fur. "You're very welcome," she whispered into her silky ear.

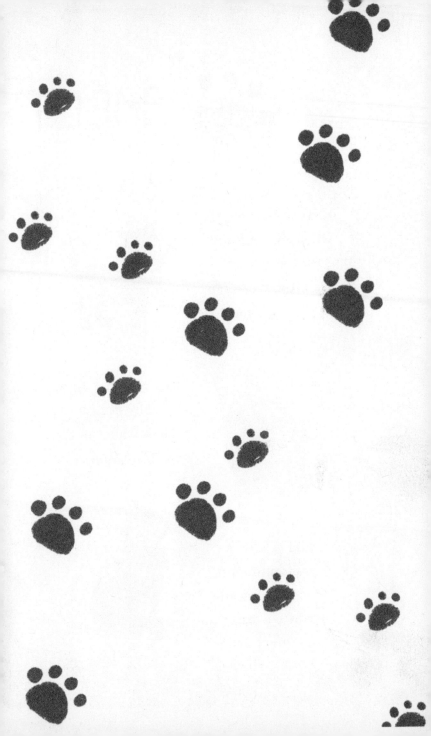

# MEET

Kitty

Kitty is a little girl who can magically turn into a cat! She is the Guardian of the Cat Council.

Tiger

Tiger is a big, brave tabby tomcat. He is leader of the Cat Council.

Suki

Suki is Kitty's grandmother. She can magically turn into a cat too!

THE CATS

Sooty

Sooty is a black and white cat. Her favorite food is sardines, and she doesn't like surprises.

Misty is Kitty's best cat friend. She loves snoozing in the sunshine.

Misty

Fang and Claws

Fang and Claws are Persian cats. They may seem mean at first but they really are quite friendly!

FELINE FACTS

Here are some fun facts about our **purrrfect** animal friends that you might like to know ...

1.

A cat's **whiskers** help them to roam around in the dark!

2.

Queen Victoria owned two Persian cats just like Claws and Fang.

3.

One cat has made it into **space**! The name of the only feline space explorer was "Félicette."

4.

Cats love to sleep. By the time a cat is nine it has slept for **six years**.

5.

When a cat is excited to see you, its tail **vibrates**!

Kitty's best friend has
a brand-new kitten!

But Misty is too scared to go outside.

Can Kitty use her magic and help
Misty to be braver?

Read on for a glimpse of
Kitty's first-ever adventure . . .

"Grandma! Grandma!" shouted Kitty Kimura excitedly. "A postcard's arrived from Mom and Dad!"

Kitty ran to the kitchen. Emails were nice, but she loved getting real mail! The card had a picture of a waving ceramic cat on it. In Japan, it was a sign of good luck. Her parents were in Japan again now.

Grandma was pouring tea into her

flowery cup. She smiled as Kitty read the short message aloud and then stuck the postcard on the fridge.

Kitty's grandma was born in Japan, but moved to the United States when Kitty's dad was little. Kitty's parents now owned a shop that sold special Japanese things, and Kitty loved all the silky kimonos, colorful fans, and sparkly cell phone charms. Three times a year, her parents went to Tokyo to look for new things for the shop.

Grandma lived with Kitty and her parents, so they spent lots of time together, especially when Mom and Dad were away. Kitty missed them, but she loved being with Grandma. She and Grandma even looked alike, with

the same dark-colored eyes. But Kitty's hair was long and black, while Grandma's bob had a streak of pure white on one side of her head.

"What shall we do for the rest of the week, Kitty-cat?" Grandma said.

Kitty's real name was Koemi, but

she loved cats so much that she was given the nickname Kitty, and now everyone called her that!

Just as Kitty was about to answer, the phone rang.

"I'll get it," Kitty offered, running into the living room.

She picked up the phone. "Hello?"

"Kitty!" said an eager voice. "It's me, Jenny!"

Kitty was surprised. Jenny was her best friend, but they hardly ever called each other, because Jenny lived only three houses away. "Hi!" she replied.

"Can you come to my house for a sleep-over tonight?" Jenny burst out. "I have something really exciting to show you!"

Kitty giggled. Jenny was always

cheerful, but today she sounded even happier than usual. "What is it?" she asked.

Jenny paused for a second. "Well . . . I was going to keep it a surprise until you got here, but I can't wait. I've got a kitten!"

Kitty gasped. "Jenny, you're so lucky!" she said, a smile spreading over her face. "Why didn't you tell me before?"

"I didn't know until today!" Jenny explained. Kitty could hear her friend bouncing up and down excitedly. "Mom kept it a surprise until I got home from school. My aunt Megan is moving to England and she couldn't take her kitten with her—so she's given Misty to me! Wait till you see her, Kitty. She's gorgeous. She's pale gray with darker gray stripes. Mom says she's a silver tabby. And I think she likes me already. As soon as Aunt Megan brought her over, she ran straight up to me and rubbed herself all around my ankles!"

"I can't believe it," Kitty said wistfully. "I *love* cats."

"I know! That's why I called you right away," Jenny replied. "It'll be as if she's your cat too! So can you come? We can play with Misty all evening!"

"Let me ask Grandma," Kitty told her friend. "I'll call you right back!"

She put down the phone and raced back into the kitchen. "Grandma!" she called breathlessly. "Can I sleep over at Jenny's house tonight? She just got a *kitten*!"

Grandma put down her teacup. "A kitten?" she replied slowly. "Well, that's lovely for Jenny . . . but, Kitty, you know you start to sneeze as soon as you're anywhere near a cat."

Kitty bit her lip. It was true. Ever since she was a baby she had been allergic to cats. It made her feel sad and a little angry, because cats were her favorite animals in the whole world. She loved their bright eyes, their silky fur, and the soft rumble of their purring.

Most of all, she liked imagining what the cats in her village got up to at night, when people were fast asleep! What made it even harder was that cats seemed to really like *her*, too. They always followed her down the street, rubbing their soft heads against her ankles and meowing eagerly. Kitty couldn't resist bending down to stroke them, but she always ended up with sore eyes and a runny nose.

"Oh, please, Grandma," she begged. "I'll take lots of tissues, and if I start to get itchy eyes or a tickly nose, I'll stop playing with Misty right away, I promise."

Grandma gazed thoughtfully at Kitty. "Well, maybe you are old enough now," she murmured softly, with the hint of a smile on her lips.

"What do you mean, Grandma?" asked Kitty, frowning. *Old enough that my allergy will be gone?* she thought, confused.

"Never mind," Grandma told her, shaking her head. "Wait here, sweetheart. I have something for you."

Kitty bit her lip, curious. Grandma sometimes acted a bit strangely. She took long naps at funny times, and she would stay up late, saying she was watching her favorite TV programs. But now she was behaving even more oddly than normal.

When Grandma came back, she placed something carefully into Kitty's hands. It was a slim silver chain with a small charm hanging from it. At first Kitty thought there were Japanese symbols on it. But as she looked more closely, she saw it was a tiny picture of a cat.

"Wow," breathed Kitty, slipping the necklace over her head. "It's beautiful."

Grandma smiled and reached under her blue silk scarf to show Kitty a matching necklace. "I have one too," she explained. "They have been in our family for a long time. Yours belonged to your great grandmother. I've been keeping it safe until the right moment. It's very precious, and I know you will take good care of it. Make sure you wear it at Jenny's house. I think it will help with your allergies."

"You mean . . . I'm allowed to go?" cried Kitty. "Thank you, Grandma!" Kitty flung her arms around Grandma, though she was puzzled about what she'd said about the necklace. How could a piece of jewelry stop her from sneezing? But she was too excited to ask questions. She was going for a sleepover at her best friend's house, and she was going to play with a sweet little kitten!

Half an hour later, Kitty and Grandma set off for Jenny's house, swinging Kitty's overnight bag between them. As soon as Kitty pressed the doorbell, the door burst open. Jenny's freckled face was flushed pink with excitement. "I couldn't wait for you to get here!" she said with a grin. "Quick—come and meet Misty!"

Jenny led them into the kitchen, where Jenny's mom and little brother, Barney, were painting. Jenny's mom washed her hands and made a cup of tea for Grandma. Kitty looked around eagerly for Misty. "Where is she?"

"Over there, on the windowsill!" said Jenny.

Kitty gasped as she spotted the little cat. "Oh, she's *so cute!*" she cried.

Misty was curled cozily in a beam of warm sunshine. She was a soft gray color, with darker gray stripes all over her body, and long silver whiskers. Her eyes were a pretty blue. When she spotted the girls, she sat straight up, pricked her ears, and gave a happy mew.

"She loves this sunny spot," Jenny said, reaching out to pat Misty's head. "Come and stroke her. She likes being tickled right here, between her ears."

Grandma was watching out of the corner of her eye. Kitty touched Misty's soft, warm head gingerly, feeling excited butterflies fill her tummy. Misty closed her eyes and purred happily as Kitty stroked her all the way down to her long tail.

"She feels like silk," whispered Kitty.

"I know. I love her so much. I still can't believe she's mine!" said Jenny, scooping Misty gently into her arms for a cuddle.

Kitty sighed. "You're the luckiest girl in the world, Jenny. I wish I wasn't allergic to cats. Then maybe Mom and Dad would let me have one too!"

Jenny raised her eyebrows. "Oh gosh—I'd forgotten about that," she said. "Are you feeling all right at the moment?"

But before Kitty could answer, Jenny's mom came over. "You're allergic, Kitty?" she asked worriedly. "I didn't know that. Are you sure you'll be okay?"

Kitty nodded quickly. "It's just a little tickle in my nose sometimes, that's all. I feel completely fine!" she said. Although at that very moment, she felt a twitch and her eyes began to tingle. She *really* wanted to rub them, but she ignored it. If Jenny's mom knew how bad her allergies could get,

Kitty knew she'd say they shouldn't have the sleepover. Even worse, she might never be able to stay at Jenny's house again!

"What do you think, Mrs. Kimura?" asked Jenny's mom, turning to

Grandma. "I've promised Jenny that Misty can sleep in her bedroom, but I don't want Kitty to feel poorly in the night."

Kitty noticed Grandma glancing at the silver necklace. *Please don't change your mind now!* she thought desperately.

But to her relief, Grandma smiled. "I think Kitty will be just fine," she said.

"All right, then," said Jenny's mom. "No staying up late, though, girls. You know it's a special treat to have a sleep-over on a weeknight." She added with a smile, "I'll take both girls to school tomorrow, Mrs. Kimura."

Jenny and Kitty grinned at each other. Now they had the whole evening to play with Misty—and a little bit of tomorrow morning!

Grandma finished her cup of tea and thanked Jenny's mom. Kitty thought Grandma gave her an especially long, tight hug goodbye, but she wasn't sure why.

Once Grandma had left, Jenny said, "Let's go to my room. I can show you all the special toys we've bought for Misty!"

They dashed up the stairs with Misty still curled up in Jenny's arms. She let Misty jump down onto the floor, and the beautiful tabby rubbed her pink nose against Jenny's leg, then started padding around, sniffing things.

"She explores by smelling everything," Jenny explained. "Aunt Megan said a cat's sense of smell is ten times better than ours! And they can see in the dark and hear much better than people too."

She picked up a squishy ball of pink wool and gave it a shake. Misty paused for a moment, her ears twitching. Then she leaped playfully at the ball, swiping it with her paw and knocking it from Jenny's hand. It rolled along the carpet, the wool unfurling as Misty chased it gleefully. Jenny and Kitty giggled. "She's so cute!" Kitty said.

They played with Misty for the rest of the evening. Even when Jenny's mom called them for dinner, Misty followed the girls downstairs and padded around their feet as they ate,

looking up at them hopefully. Afterward, they chose a movie to watch in the living room. When they settled on the sofa, Misty hopped gracefully onto Kitty's lap, gave a friendly meow, and curled up in a fluffy ball.

"She really likes you!" Jenny told Kitty.

Kitty beamed and stroked Misty's velvety ears. She felt really lucky that Jenny was so nice about sharing Misty. And she felt even luckier that she had a new cat-friend! The only problem was her allergies. She tried not to think about the strange itchiness in her nose and eyes, but the more time she spent with Misty, the worse it got. By the time the movie finished, it was almost like her whole *body* felt odd!

Before she scrambled into her sleeping bag on Jenny's bedroom floor, Kitty pulled a packet of tissues out of her overnight bag and tucked them under her pillow. She hoped she wouldn't sneeze too much during the night.

Jenny dived into bed and Misty jumped onto the bedcovers to snuggle up by her feet.

"Sleep tight, girls!" called Jenny's mom, switching off the light.

"Goodnight, Kitty!" Jenny whispered happily. "Today has been the best day ever!"

"I know! Night night," Kitty whispered back. Before long, she was drifting into sleep.

Kitty's eyes flew open. It was very quiet in Jenny's bedroom. Moonlight was shining through a gap in the curtains. She knew right away what had woken her up: her nose was tickling like crazy!

She rubbed it, but it didn't help. In fact, that only made it worse—now her cheeks were itching and her ears were tingling. Suddenly, Kitty noticed the tickly feeling was spreading. The tips of her fingers and toes felt like they were full of fizzy bubbles, and there was a strange prickling all over her arms and legs. Finally, she began to sneeze. "Achoo! Achoo! *Aaaaa*choo!"

The bubbly, tickly feeling spread right through her, and it felt like her whole body was sparkling and glowing. Kitty gave one more enormous sneeze. "AAAAAAAACHOOOOO!"

When she opened her eyes again,

everything felt different. Her nose had stopped itching and her eyes weren't sore anymore—but something was strange about them. *I must have gotten used to the darkness*, she thought. *I can see everything much more clearly!*

Then Kitty thought something else was odd. Jenny's bed was much bigger and farther away. *How is that possible?* Kitty wondered. She looked around, and as her gaze drifted down, she stared in amazement. Where her hands had been before, there were now two small, furry black paws.

Cat paws.

Kitty cried out in shock—but the sound that came out wasn't a cry. It was a meow.

Ella Moonheart grew up telling fun and exciting stories to anyone who would listen. Now that she's an author, she's thrilled to be able to tell stories to so many more children with her Kitty's Magic books. Ella loves animals, but cats most of all! She wishes she could turn into one just like Kitty, but she's happy to just play with her pet cat, Nibbles—when she's not writing her books, of course!